John Goodwin

Published in association with
The Basic Skills Agency

Hodder & Stoughton

A MEMBER OF THE HODDER HEADLINE GROUP

Acknowledgements
Cover: Barry Downard
Illustrations: Ben Hasler

Orders: please contact Bookpoint Ltd, 130 Milton Park, Abingdon, Oxon OX14 4SB. Telephone: (44) 01235 827720, Fax: (44) 01235 400454. Lines are open from 9.00–6.00, Monday to Saturday, with a 24 hour message answering service. You can also order through our website: www.hodderheadline.co.uk.

British Library Cataloguing in Publication Data
A catalogue record for this title is available from The British Library

ISBN 0 340 87662 X

First published 2003
Impression number 10 9 8 7 6 5 4 3 2 1
Year 2009 2008 2007 2006 2005 2004 2003

Typeset by SX Composing DTP, Rayleigh, Essex.
Printed in Great Britain for Hodder & Stoughton Educational, a division of Hodder Headline, 338 Euston Road, London NW1 3BH by Athenaeum Press, Gateshead, Tyne and Wear.

Contents

1
A Dream for the Future

I'm standing at the top of the ramp.
I hear the skateboard wheels rolling.

Faster and faster.
Down the slope.
They then zoom up the other side.

Skaters shimmy.
They make neat flicks.
Then they're up in the air.
Flying high.
Landing smartly on top of the ramp.
Then down again.

That's what I dream of.
Day and night.
Skating at our own
skateboard park.

We're going to call it:
'Sk8'
A cool name.

Sk8 isn't built yet.
But it soon will be.
Any time now.

2
The Council Meeting

The village hall was packed.
The council had organised a meeting.
It was to decide if we were going
to have the skateboard park.

Loads of kids were there.
Some parents were too.
Other adults from the town
made up the rest.
I was sitting next to Karlie.
My best mate.
'This is it,' I said to her.
'Tonight they'll vote for Sk8.'

They asked for kids to speak first.
I got to my feet straight away.
I said my name loud and clear.
'I'm Ben,' I said.
'All the kids round here
want this skateboard park.
It will give us something to do.
Somewhere to go.
A place for us.'

Then Karlie got to her feet.
'We've even given the park
a name,' she said.
'We're going to call it Sk8.'

Karlie was going to say
something else.
But she didn't get a chance.

Somebody spoke from the other side
of the hall.
It was a very loud adult voice.
'That park should never
be built,' he shouted.
'We don't want it round here.'

Then other loud voices joined in.
'It will cause nothing but trouble,'
they shouted.
'This isn't the kind of place
for a skateboard park.
'Build it somewhere else.'

There was more shouting.
'Yes, build it somewhere else.'
People started arguing.
Pointing fingers.
Stamping their feet.
Waving their arms about.

The shouting was louder than ever.
They had to close the meeting.

I wanted to walk home with Karlie.
To talk about what had happened.
But her dad grabbed her arm.
'Karlie is coming home
with me,' he said.
I walked home alone.
I tried to work out what would
happen next.

3
A Setback

The following day, I phoned Karlie.
'Are you coming out?' I asked her.

'I can't,
My dad won't let me,' she said.
'He doesn't want me to get
into trouble.'

'What trouble?' I asked

'He says the skateboard park
means trouble,' she said.
'He says it will never be built.
It's caused bad feeling in the town.'

I felt myself go red in the face.
How could he say the park
would never be built?
Then Karlie said,
'My dad's just come in.
I've got to go.
Bye, Ben.'

I didn't see Karlie for two weeks.
Then she phoned me up.
'Ben,' she said.
'I can't speak for too long.
But I'll meet you by the field,
in 20 minutes. Is that OK?'

Too right it was OK.
I grabbed my bike.
I cycled up to the open field.
The place where we hoped to have
our skateboard park.
Karlie stood by the gate of the field.
She looked sad.

I climbed off my bike.
'What's wrong?' I asked.

'This,' she said.
She pointed to a small pink notice
on the gate.

'We've lost, Ben,' she said.

'What do you mean?' I asked.

'The notice says it all.
They're going to build a park here.
But it's not a skateboard park.
It's going to be a car park,'
she said.

I read the notice twice.
We'd lost one battle for sure.
But the fight would go on.
We wouldn't give up.
Oh no. We'd never do that.

NOTICE

4

P is for Protest

We began to plan.
Karlie phoned Katy.
Katy phoned Lin Sue.
Lin Sue phoned Sam
and Zak and Tom.
I phoned Joe and Josh and Eliza.
Eliza phoned very many more.

We all talked and met.
Then we talked some more.
At last we were ready.

We chose Saturday.
The first day of Plan P.
P is for Protest.

The shopping mall was busy.
There were hundreds of shoppers.
Crowded car parks.
People eager to shop.
Or ready to climb into their cars.
Heading for home.

There were five car parks.
We hit them all.

Kids on skateboards.
Zooming into the mall car parks.
Flipping over kerbs.
Flying down ramps.
Blocking off traffic.
Causing trouble.
Creating chaos.

Each kid had a message painted
on their back:
'Our town needs a skate park.'
'Sk8 for US.'
'Say "NO" to a new car park.'
'Kids need your vote.'
'Join us now.'

It was the same in other car parks.
All over the town.
We didn't miss one.

A week went by.
I thought people would be
talking about us.
That we'd be in the local newspaper.
Or even on local radio.
None of that happened.
There was just silence.

We might as well have
stayed at home.

5
Front Page News

The next week, we went for Plan P2.
This time there were more of us.
We also chose a new place
to protest.
Somewhere very different.

Our protest had to be an afternoon
after school.
Right in the middle of town
at the biggest building around.

At 4.15 pm, we phoned the local papers
to say where we'd be.
At 4.16 pm, the skateboard wheels
began to roll.
Out in the car park at first.
We waited for an adult
to enter the building.
Any adult would do.
Then we followed them in
through the opened door.
Right into the town hall.
The home of the council.
Huge, flat marble floors.
Perfect for skateboarding.

We took them by surprise.
Nobody stopped us.
Everyone was gobsmacked.
Seeing so many kids on skateboards.
We skated along the corridor.
Right up to the big meeting room.

We burst into the room.
The council members were in the middle
of a meeting.
We gave them our letter of protest.
It said how sad we were not to have
our skateboard park.
It asked them to change their minds.

At first,
the members didn't know what to do.
Then they called security.
Security chucked us out.

But the newspaper covered our story.
We had our photos on the front page.
I phoned Karlie when I saw the paper.
Her dad answered her mobile.
He was so angry.
He said to keep away from Karlie.
'She doesn't want to be with
a troublemaker like you,' he said.
Then he switched off her phone.

6
A Dream Comes True

A member of the council spoke
on local radio.
She said our protest was
a waste of time.
The field was going to be a car park.
Nothing could stop that.

The same day Lin Sue phoned me.
She said her dad has his own field.
We could use that as
a skateboard park.
Did we want it?
You bet we did.

There was only one problem.
We could use the field for free,
but we needed money for the fence
and ramps.

So we washed cars.
We did a sponsored swim.
Our parents did a raffle.
At last we were ready.

One Saturday, we all went to the field.
Even Karlie managed to sneak away
from home.

Eliza's dad got everyone organised.
He works with wood in his job.
We cut and drilled the wood.
We rolled out the metal fence wire.
The wood grew into four
giant frames.
The fence wire grew tall and strong.

Everybody pulled and lifted
together.
It was a field no longer.
At last, it was our skateboard park.
Zak's painted sign,
'Sk8'
was fixed to the wire fence.
Then the wheels started to roll.
Faster and faster.
Down the slope.

Neat flicks.
Shimmies.
Bodies on boards.

Flying high.
Up in the air.
Landing smartly.
Top of the ramp.
Then down again.

A dream come true.

7
The Vandal Unmasked

Sk8 was open house.
Anybody could come and skate.
That was our rule.
So long as there was no trouble.
Everybody was welcome.
It was free to all.

Big kids.
Little kids.
Dads.
Mums.
Grans.
Nobody was shut out.

It was busy sometimes.
But it worked.
There was never any trouble.

That is until one Friday night.
We went to the park straight
after school.
Karlie and me.

We saw it straight away.
A corner of the wire fence had been
torn down.
Part of the wooden ramp had been
burnt to the ground.
We were gutted.
Both of us too sick to speak.

Later we began to ask questions
'Who could have done
a thing like this?'
'Why did they try to wreck it?'

The police were called.
They said, 'There's been vandalism attacks all over the town.
We think it's a gang of youths.'
They didn't catch the vandals.
We still didn't know who'd tried to wreck Sk8.

It took us weeks and weeks.
We rebuilt the ramp.
We mended the fence.
Wheels once more zoomed down the ramps.
We put a big padlock on the gate, when it wasn't in use.

Karlie and I kept our eyes on the place.
We checked it out each day after school.

One day,
we saw something was wrong again.
'Look, there's smoke,' said Karlie.
We ran fast.
The padlock had been
smashed open.
We could just see the head of a person
over the top of the ramp.
Karlie put her finger over her lip.
'Ssh,' she whispered.
Together we crept closer.

The figure had its back towards us.
A petrol can was in its hand.
'Stop that!' I shouted out.
The figure turned towards us.

Karlie cried out.
It was not a loud shout.
But a low moan.
She knew the figure with the petrol can.
It was her own father.

Once again, Sk8 is packed with
zooming skaters.
You wouldn't know that the ramp
had been repaired twice.
I go there sometimes.
It's not so much fun now.
Karlie and her dad have moved away.
Gone to live in another town.

People have forgotten what he did.
Not me.
I'll never forget.